TITLE II-A

My Dad Lives in a

Downtown Hotel

MY DAD LIVES IN A DOWNTOWN HOTEL

Written by
Peggy Mann

Illustrated by
Richard Cuffari

Doubleday & Company, Inc.
Garden City, New York

FOR MY FRIEND
Miriam Chaikin

ISBN: 0-385-07080-2 Trade
0-385-08784-5 Prebound
Library of Congress Catalog Card Number 72-90049
Text Copyright © 1973 Peggy Mann
Illustrations Copyright © 1973 Richard Cuffari
All Rights Reserved.
Printed in the United States of America
9 8 7 6 5 4 3 2

1

When I got to school that morning I wondered whether anyone would notice anything different about me. I sure *felt* different, I can tell you that.

But I guess no one noticed anything. Except Miss Clifford.

During recess she sent me into the supply room where they keep the basketballs and volleyball nets and things. "What's got into you today, Joey?" she said. "Running around, shoving into everyone! You'd better stay in here till you feel you can behave yourself. And then come out."

She closed the door hard behind her.

I looked around. I felt like knocking

over everything in the stupid supply room. Ripping the posters off the walls. Busting my fists through the volleyball nets. Throwing the equipment all over the place. But then I figured what was the sense. It would only make Miss Clifford trouble. And it wasn't *her* fault that my dad had walked out on my mom and me last night.

So I just sat there on a cardboard carton staring at the wall. I felt like my whole insides were burning up with hate for my dad. I mean, what did he want to do such a terrible thing for? Didn't he love us, or what?

Suddenly I thought of that time he was trying to teach me to swim. He didn't hold me and let me kick my legs, like I've seen other dads do. He just picked me up and threw me off the pier into the water. "Sink or swim, Joey!" he called after me.

Well, I managed to make it back to the steps of the pier. But I mean maybe he *wanted* me to sink. Maybe he wanted to get rid of me even way back then.

Maybe that was why he walked out last night. He just couldn't take me any more.

I hoped very hard no one would come busting into the supply room just then.

I mean I was squeezing my teeth together. And squeezing my eyes tight closed. But even so, tears kept leaking out.

Maybe if I promised my dad that I'd get good—maybe then he'd come back.

All of a sudden I knew exactly what to do.

I'd make out a list of all the things I do that he doesn't like. Then I'd go down to his office. Right away. This afternoon. I'd give him the list and promise not to do any of those things again. Then I'd ask him to take me back home. And then he'd *be* home. And that'd be the end of it.

There was a clipboard hanging on a nail in the supply room. It had sheets of yellow paper and a pencil attached to it by a string. Miss Clifford uses it to keep score for basketball games and things. But I used it now for making my list. And somehow even just writing down all those bad things I do made me feel a little better.

That afternoon when school was out, instead of going home like usual, I borrowed some money from Pepe Gonzales. He's two classes ahead of me. But I know him from the bus. We sit together a lot.

Probably he wouldn't even talk to me if it wasn't we happen to go home the same

4

way on the bus. I mean Pepe's one of the best basketball players in the school. Even though he's short. And the youngest one on the team.

I asked Pepe for the money because he's the only one I know that's working right now. He's got a job working after school in a grocery store. The store doesn't pay him, because he's too young. But when he delivers groceries to people they give him tips. Sometimes he makes a dollar a day. I mean, he's loaded.

Pepe even gave me ten cents extra in case I wanted to buy myself something on the way.

I took the bus downtown. I was kind of scared because I didn't know exactly where to get off. Before, when Dad took me to his office, I never paid too much attention to how I was getting there.

I kept staring out the window at the traffic and the tall buildings, trying to recognize the place. But after a while I forgot about remembering where to get off. I started thinking all over again how it had been last night.

I mean, they used to fight soft.
Even when I'd lie in bed *trying* to make

out what they were saying, I couldn't. All I could ever hear were these kind of hissing whispers.

But *last* night! If you want to know, last night I really tried hard *not* to hear them! For a while I held the pillow around my ears like my head was some kind of sandwich. I couldn't hear the words then. But the *sound* of the words was what counted. And even the pillow couldn't shut out that sound.

Suddenly I heard their bedroom door open. And slam shut. And I heard my dad stomping down the hall, across the living room. Then I heard the front door open. And slam shut.

Everything was quiet. Spooky quiet.

I got up and opened the door of my room, just a crack. All I could see was the dark hallway. The door to my mom and dad's room was still shut. Should I go in there? I was planning to. But somehow I found myself running across the living room. I opened the front door and went into the outside hallway. No one was there. That pointer thing above the elevator was going down—4, 3, 2, 1. Then it stopped. I waited awhile for the elevator

to come back up to our floor. With my dad in it. Finally I pressed the button. The elevator came up. But when the door slid open no one came out. The elevator was empty.

I started to shiver. That hallway was cold. I had no slippers on or anything, only my pajamas.

Probably my dad just got very mad and stormed out of the house to take a walk and cool off his temper. I'd seen that happen on the TV. The guy gets mad and slams out of the house. So what if my dad never did that before? There's always a first time, isn't there?

I went back to the apartment. Should I go in and see my mom? Everything was still spooky quiet in there. Then I heard a little sound like she was trying not to cry.

What would I do if I went in there and she *was* crying, for God's sake?

I went back into my own room, closed the door, and got into bed, I burrowed down deep under the covers because I still was shivering. After a while I got warmed up. But still, I didn't sleep much.

Did you ever feel too scared even to *think* about what you're scared of? That's the worst kind of scared there is.

Then—at breakfast the next morning—I found out what it was I was scared about. I found out about it after Mom burned the toast.

Our toaster doesn't work too good. It doesn't pop up like it's supposed. So when you figure the toast is ready, you have to unplug the toaster and dig out the toast with a fork.

The first round, Mom forgot about, till I smelled it. She threw those burned pieces into the garbage. And put in two more slices of bread. But this time she forgot to unplug the toaster and when she stuck the fork in she got an electric shock. It must have been a pretty terrible shock, because she began to cry.

I didn't know *what* to do. I mean, did *you* ever see your mom cry? It's terrible.

If *you* cry, she knows what to do. She takes you in her lap and kind of cuddles you. Even if you're really too big for that, still it feels okay.

But if your mom cries, what are *you* going to do? Take her on *your* lap?

First I just stood there, looking at her. I mean, she was really sobbing, you know? Gasping and sobbing, with her two hands over her mouth like she was trying to hold

9

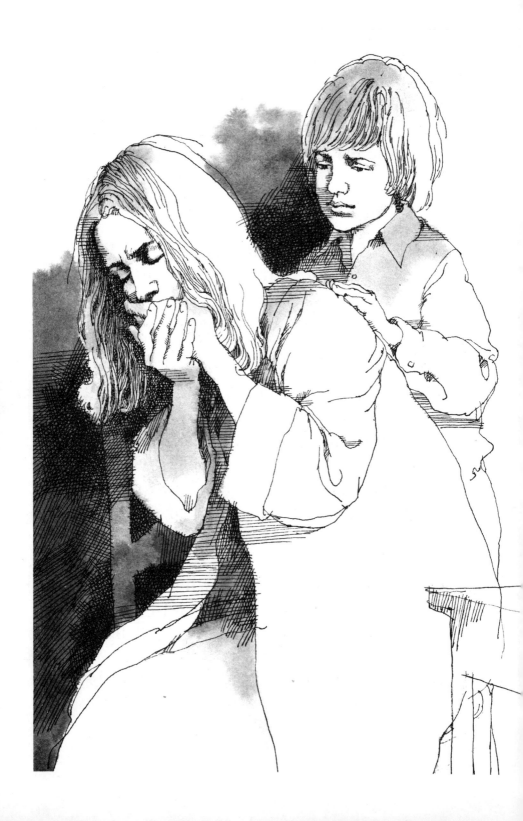

it all back. But the tears wouldn't stop crying out of her eyes.

Finally I said, "Don't, Mom." Then I said, "Listen, Mom, we don't need any old toast this morning anyway."

But she didn't stop.

So I decided to do the same as if *I* was crying. I climbed into her lap. And she cuddled me.

It worked. After a little while she stopped crying.

"Listen," I said then, "we better wake Dad up. He'll be late for work."

I'd kept thinking to myself: *He's still sleeping. He was out late walking around the streets. And now he's tired. That's why he*

didn't come for breakfast yet. He's still sleeping.

Somehow I *knew* he wasn't in the house any more. But I didn't *believe* it until my mom said it out into words: "Daddy isn't here."

I said, "Well, where is he?"

Mom took a dish towel from the back of the kitchen chair. She wiped the tears off her face. Then she started telling me.

It was like a speech she'd been rehearsing over and over. She said the words pretty fast. And it didn't sound like Mom talking at all. "Joey —" she said, "there are some people who just don't seem to get on together. Each one may be perfectly fine as a person. But when the two are married — well, it — doesn't work, that's all. So the sensible thing for those people to do is to — well, break it up. Not live together any more."

She stopped talking. I didn't want to hear any more anyway. I got off her lap. "Listen, Mom," I said, "are you going to get me any breakfast, or aren't you? I'll be late to school."

She jumped up quick, like she was glad to be doing something. And not talking any more. She made me scrambled eggs, soft like I like them. And hot chocolate.

(Usually, I don't get *that* except on Sunday.) And two pieces of toast done just right, with butter melting on them.

As I was eating I thought about telling her maybe Dad would want to stay with us if she made *him* a good breakfast like this every morning.

But I ended up not saying anything about it. Because even though the eggs were just how I like them, I hardly ate any. I didn't feel too hungry.

"Joey," my mom kept saying, "please eat something. You can't go off to school with nothing in your stomach."

But there was like a clump of tears blocking up my throat. So how could I swallow scrambled eggs?

That clump of tears stuck there all through the day. Even now, in the bus, I could feel it.

Suddenly the bus gave a kind of lurch. And it lurched me out of remembering. Back to where I was.

But where *was* I?

I'd been staring out the window all that time. But not seeing anything.

"What street are we on?" I said to the lady sitting next to me.

"Fifteenth Street," she told me.

Fifteenth Street! My dad's office was on Forty-something Street. We must have driven right past Downtown!

I pulled at the cord which makes the little bell cling that you want to get off. And when the bus stopped at Fourteenth Street I did get off—quick.

I was on a big wide sidewalk with a lot of stores and neon lights flashing even though it was bright daylight. And people hurrying along. No kids, though. I didn't see a kid anywhere on the whole street.

I mean, I never felt so little in my life.

2

I didn't know which way to walk. Uptown or downtown. Right or left. Back or forth.

All these strangers were hurrying by. I thought about going up to someone; asking the way to Downtown where my dad's office building is. But the bus had taken me *past* Downtown. So maybe here my dad's office would be called Uptown.

Anyway, no one looked very friendly. So I decided not to ask.

I stood for a while staring in a store window at ladies' shoes. And I kept chewing at my lip because sometimes that can stop you from crying. It didn't work too good though. I had this five-cent pack of Kleenex in my pocket. Mom always stuffs a pack there before I go to school. She's real gone on those little packs of Kleenex. I used up the whole pack blowing my nose and wiping at tears. Then I had to just sniffle.

Suddenly I started hating my dad all over again. It was *his* fault that I was lost. If he hadn't walked out on me and Mom—

Then, remembering Mom, I knew what to do!

Why hadn't I thought of that simple thing before? I guess sometimes troubles make you stupid.

All I had to do was phone Mom up and ask *her* the way to Dad's office!

There was a luncheonette next to the shoe store. They had a telephone on the wall right by the front window. Not in a booth or anything. Just out where everyone eating lunch could hear all your business. But I felt in such a hurry to talk to Mom that I didn't want to wait till I found a more private phone.

I went inside.

The place smelled like pizza. That smell always makes me hungry even when I'm not. But this time I was. I'd hardly eaten any breakfast or any lunch. But if I bought a piece of pizza I wouldn't have enough money to get to my dad's office. So I just kind of swallowed, and went to the telephone.

It was too high up on the wall for me to reach, so I took three fat phone books from the stand and piled one on top of the other. The counterman looked at me kind of funny. But he didn't say anything. So I climbed on top of the phone books. And then I could reach okay.

I clinked the dime in. Then I dialed, very carefully. All I had left of Pepe Gonzales' money was this one dime and bus fare. If I dialed the wrong number, I'd really be stuck.

"Hello," my mom said.

I felt so glad to hear her that I couldn't say anything at all.

"Hello!" my mom said again in a funny kind of screamy way.

"Hi, Mom," I said.

"JOEY! Where *are* you? I've been frantic!"

"I'm on Fourteenth Street," I said.

"What are you doing on Fourteenth Street? I was all ready to call the police!"

The *police!* She really must be a little off

the beam right now. Who calls the police when a kid is half an hour late from school? But to be honest I felt kind of pleased that she was so worried about me.

Then, right away, I felt ashamed. After all, Mom turned down a good full-time job at the store on account of me. She told them she *wanted* her part-time job so she could be home when I got back from school every day. And I hadn't even thought of phoning to tell her that I'd be late. God! Maybe she thought *I'd* walked out on her too!

I didn't want to explain everything on the phone because after all there were people sitting close on the counter stools. And I sure didn't want *them* listening in to all these private things. So I just said, "Listen, Mom, I'm going to Dad's office. But I forgot the address."

"Oh—Joey!" It sounded like she might start to cry, so I said, real quick, "Mom, everything'll be okay. If you only tell me the address of Dad's office."

"Tell me where *you* are, Joey," she said. "I'll come right down and I'll take you there."

"Listen, Mom," I said, "this is something private between me and Dad. I got a contract I wrote and everything. If *you* come along—" I broke off. I didn't want all those stool people hearing any more.

My mom didn't say anything.

"Listen, Mom," I said, "after he reads my contract I'll get Dad to bring me home. And then he'll *be* home. And that'll be the end of it."

"You're—sure you can find the way, Joey?" She said the words very slow. But like she thought it might be a good idea.

"Sure I'm sure." I told her. Even though I didn't feel so sure at all. Then I saw a police car driving by outside. "Listen," I said, "there's a policeman right out the door. I'll ask him to put me on the right bus and everything."

"Well," my mom said, "—all right." And she told me the address. She even made me get out my school notebook and write it down and repeat it all over again to her. Then she said, "Joey."

"Yeah, Mom?"

"Don't forget—have your father bring you home."

"Sure, Mom," I said. "After all, that's the whole idea."

And I hung up.

When I got outside, the police car was gone.

I saw a bus stop and walked over to it. Then I thought I'd better make sure it was the right bus stop. There was a fat lady standing next to me. I sort of pulled at her sleeve a little, and when she looked down I showed her my notebook with the address written in it.

She said, "Honey, if you get on this bus that's coming you'll end up at the Hudson River."

She tried to explain how to get to the bus stop I wanted. But I guess I looked as mixed up as I felt, because she suddenly said, "Come on with me, child." And she shifted all her packages into one arm so she could take my hand like I was three years old or something. She led me across a big wide street with traffic coming every which-a-way. And finally we got to another bus stop.

"I'll wait with you," she said.

Then she asked what I was doing down here all by myself.

And—I told her! I mean, this perfectly strange lady—I told her all about my dad walking out on my mom and me last night.

When I got done telling she just nodded and said, "Well, it happens." She didn't

sound too surprised. Then she asked if I had enough money. I showed her the dimes I had left. And — would you believe it — she put two quarters in my hand. "Just in case you don't find your dad," she said. "This way you'll have money to get back home again."

The bus pulled up then. Before I could even ask where she lived so as I could send the money back, she kind of shoved me up the bus steps and called out to the driver, "See that this boy gets out at Forty-eighth Street."

I plunked in my money. Then I looked out the window. She was still there, waiting to see me off. She smiled and waved. Just like she was a longtime friend. In fact, I *felt* like she was. And I didn't even know her name.

I went up to the bus conductor then and showed *him* the address in my composition book. Just to make sure. And I sat myself right in the front seat where he could see me, to keep reminded.

The buildings grew taller and taller as we drove up into Downtown. And finally the driver said, "Next stop is yours, sonny."

I got off quick. Ran across the street. And suddenly I felt my right age again. And my right size. Because I recognized my dad's office building.

It's a tall building, and the elevator zoops up so fast it makes your ears kind of pop. I got out at the twenty-third floor and walked into the reception room.

The girl at the reception desk was new.

Every time before when I'd visited Dad's office they had that old Miss Simpson sitting there. She always wanted to take me on her lap, which I wouldn't have liked to do anyway. But in her case it was worse because she had smelly breath.

When I was real little there was nothing I could do about it because Dad would just pick me up and plop me on her lap. "Well, here's your boyfriend to see you, Grace," he'd say. Or something gooney like that. And then she'd squeeze me and hug me and call me her little schnookypook and tell me how big I'd grown and why didn't I come to see her more often.

Anyway, this time she wasn't there. Maybe she died or something.

They had this pretty girl with red hair, and she looked at me with a nice little kind of smile when I got off the elevator. "Can I help you?" she said.

I told her I would like to see Mr. Joseph Grant.

"Whom shall I say is calling?"

"His son."

"Well!" She gave me a bigger smile. "So *you're* Joey!" She rang through on the switchboard. "Mr. Grant," she said. "Mr. Joseph Grant, Junior, is here to see you."

Then she turned back to me. "He'll be right out."

And he was! By the time I had sat myself down in the armchair and picked up a magazine—he was there. He came charging through the doorway into the reception room. "Joey!" he said. "What are *you* doing here?"

"I just came," I said, which was kind of a stupid thing to say. But I couldn't think of anything else.

My dad seemed sort of upset. "Wait right there, son," he said. "I'll get my coat. I'll be back in a minute. We'll go out and get an ice cream soda or something." And he was gone.

Always before when I came to his office he took me inside, introduced me to

everyone in a proud kind of laughing way. But this time he just left me sitting in the reception room. Maybe he'd already started not to love me so much.

"What's your favorite kind of ice cream?" the girl at the reception desk said.

"I dunno," I said. Actually, what I like best is chocolate chip mint. But they don't have that at most places. So usually I just settle for strawberry.

She opened her purse.

"If I give you some money would you ask your dad to bring me back a strawberry soda?"

"Well," I said, "I don't think he'll be coming back today. I mean, by the time he takes me all the way home he probably won't want to leave again to come back here."

She nodded. Then she closed her purse. "I shouldn't have an ice cream soda anyway. I'm supposed to be on a diet."

The switchboard got very busy then, so she couldn't talk to me anymore. I was just as glad. I had more important things to think about than ice cream sodas. I took out my list and studied it over.

Dear Dad

Will you come home again if I promise here with

1. Never to be frech and call you stooped any more

2. to go to bed on time so you so you don't have to haler at me any more

3. not to play the tv to loud on sunday morning when your sleeping

4. not to leave my train tracks on the living room floor

5. to do my homework with out watching the t.v.

from now on I'll try all the time to be the kind of boy you'ed like to have around. So please dad give me another chance and come home. Love from your son Joey Grant

3

We went to Schrafft's. The place was pretty empty. Just a few ladies at the tables. And some waitresses sitting in a booth at the back, eating.

Dad and I sat in a booth, too. I was glad. It was more private.

We each picked up a menu and looked at it.

There was soft music playing, and I said, "Nice music."

My dad looked up from his menu. "What?" he said.

"The music in here. It's nice."

"Oh," he said. "Yes."

A waitress came over then. She had a

black uniform and a little white apron and a friendly kind of chirpy voice. "Have you decided on your order, gentlemen?" she said.

I asked if they had chocolate chip mint ice cream. And they did. I thought that was a good sign—that *everything* would go right now, in Schrafft's. I ordered myself a Broadway soda—that's coffee and chocolate syrup mixed—with chocolate chip mint ice cream.

"I'll just have coffee," my dad said to the waitress.

She wrote down our orders on a little green pad and went away.

My dad kept looking at the menu. I don't know why, since we'd ordered already. Watching him, I got to feeling more and more scared. It was like I could feel my heart thumping into my head.

Should I pull out my list now, or what?

Then my dad put the menu away. "Well," he said, "how's school?"

How's *school?* He was talking to me like I was a son he hadn't seen for months and he had to catch up on all the news.

I didn't even bother to answer such a stupid question.

Dad nodded his head a little—like I *had*

answered. And he said, "Did your mother —talk to you this morning? About—" He sort of shrugged with his shoulders and his hands.

"Well," I said, "Yeah—well, I mean, she said—something."

"What did she tell you?"

"When are you coming home?" I said.

"I'm not."

I stared at him. I mean, how could he just sit there and say it out like that? He could have said, *I don't know*. Or, *It's something your mother and I have got to talk over*. But no, he just sits there and announces that he's not coming home!

"Look, Dad," I said, "I think I know what the trouble was. And there's something I can do about it. I can make everything okay—so you'll *want* to come home again. I promise."

I took out my list and handed it to him.

Dad read it over. He kept swallowing.

Then he folded the list carefully. "May I keep this?" he said.

"Sure, Dad. It's for you. We could even get it notarized," I didn't know what that meant exactly. But I did know it would make the paper more official. Like a real contract.

My dad put the list in his pocket. Then he did something he never did before, at least not that I could remember. He put his hand over mine and held it real hard. And he looked right straight at me.

"Son," he said, "I want you to understand something. I want you to get it very straight. This has nothing to do with you—my leaving. Nothing at all. In fact, it was *because* of you that your mom and I stayed together as long as we did. But now we figure it'd be better for you living in a house where there's peace and quiet. Instead of tension and fights all the time."

"But you and Mom fight nice and soft," I said. "So I can't even hear you. I don't mind if you fight. So what? I'm used to it."

The waitress came then with our orders. "Here you are, gentlemen," she said in her cheery voice, just like everything in the world was wonderful. She put my ice cream soda in front of me. "Will there be anything else, sir?" she said to my dad.

He shook his head.

She put the bill on the table and went away.

My dad ripped the top off a paper packet of sugar. Then he stirred the sugar into his coffee. I watched the spoon going around and around. He always takes his coffee without sugar, so I don't know why he was stirring so much.

"Don't you want your soda?" he said.

I nodded. But I didn't start sucking at the straws. I mean, I just couldn't. I'd been plenty hungry at the luncheonette. But now I wasn't at all.

Then Dad asked that same question again. "What did your mother tell you this morning?"

"Just that you—weren't there."

He frowned.

I didn't want him getting angry at Mom so I told him real quick, "I didn't *want* to hear any more."

He opened *another* packet of sugar and stirred it into his coffee. "Joey," he said, "Listen. I—you know—I love you very much. Your mom does too. Joey, nothing will ever change about that. You hear me, son?"

He looked up at me. I looked back at him. Then he started stirring again and staring into his coffee cup. "I mean, whether I'm living at home, Joey. Or in a hotel. Or even if I get married to some-one else—and have another wife—

36

nothing will ever change how I feel about you, Joey."

"What are you talking about?" I said. "How can you get married *again*? You're already married to Mom!"

He breathed in very deep. "Well," he said, "what your mother *should* have told you this morning—we're getting a divorce."

It was like even the soft music in Schrafft's had stopped playing. It was like there was this terrible shaking quiet in the whole world.

"Things will work out much better like that," my dad said. "It may not seem so right now, son. But believe me, it's true." He put his hand over mine again. "I see the circus is coming to town. How about we'll go? Just the two of us."

I looked at him.

I mean, I like the circus a lot. And I'd always *wanted* to go there just with my dad. Instead, it was Mom who took me. With Aunt Gladys and her two bratty little kids. Girls. I used to sit there *imagining* I was with my dad instead.

But now I only felt this clump of hard madness inside me. I mean, did he think a couple of circus tickets would make everything all right?

"We'll go on opening *night!*" my dad said. "Instead of the matinee. And maybe before the show we'll have dinner together. In some swell restaurant. Would you like that?"

I didn't say one word.

"Matter of fact," my dad went on, "every single Sunday you and I will go out together. Just the two of us. Do something special."

Sunday? Sure! What was he putting me on for! Sunday's his bowling day. With The Boys. The *Boys!* What a laugh! One of them's got white hair already!

"Dad," I said. "I don't *want* to go to the circus! Dad, I know there's a lot of *other* things I do that get you mad. Dad, I promise if you come home I won't ever do a single one of those things again. You can add on to that list I gave you. Make it as long as you want. I'll promise the whole works! Then you won't ever need to holler at me again. That way the house'll be real quiet if that's how you like it. Everything'll be just how you like it, Dad. I *promise!*"

He didn't say anything. He drank down

his coffee. All of it. Then he sat staring into the empty cup.

I sat, stiff. My hands were clenched in my lap. I *knew* he was going to say okay. He'd give it another try. He'd take me home, and I'd say, *Well, Mom, here we are. Home.* And that'd be that. I'd be so good he'd just *want* to come home every night. There'd be no more talk about divorce — nothing. We'd be a family again.

"Joey," my dad said, "how can I make you understand? My leaving home — it had nothing to do with anything you did. It was my fault, Joey. My fault and your mom's fault. We never should have married in the first place. Sometimes it happens like that, Joey. I mean, the woman can be great. The man can be okay, too. But they just don't — team up well, that's all. So —" He shrugged.

I started sucking at my soda. I mean, I didn't want it. But I sure didn't come all the way here to bust out crying in the middle of Schrafft's.

"Correction," my dad said. "Your mom and I *didn't* make a mistake in getting married. Because if we hadn't married, there wouldn't have been any Joey. And that would've been — *terrible*."

I looked up at him. The way he said that word—*terrible*—it kind of shot out of his mouth. Like he really meant it!

"Listen, Dad," I said, "Mom told me to tell you to be sure to bring me home. So maybe we better get going."

He frowned again. I mean, why did he have to frown every time I even *mentioned* her?

"Did your mother send you down here?" he said.

"No!" I told him. "It was *my* idea!"

He nodded. "Look, son, I— Look, I wasn't expecting you, was I? So I've got this important meeting scheduled. If I'd known you were coming, I—"

"Sure, Dad," I said real quick. "I get it."

"Look, Joey," he said, "if you'll feel better about it, I'll cancel the meeting. I'll take you home in a cab. I'll see you into the elevator. But that's all. I'll have to come right back to the office again."

"And *then* where'll you go? After the office?"

"To a hotel."

"What hotel?"

"Just some hotel. Downtown here."

"It sounds pretty crummy," I said.

"Wouldn't you rather be living at home than staying in some lousy hotel?"

My dad didn't answer. He signaled the waitress. When she came over he said, "Check, please."

"I gave you your check, sir," she said, and she pointed at it, right in front of him.

"Oh," my dad said. "Sorry."

He got up and put on his coat. I put on my coat. And suddenly we were walking out of Schrafft's. We were on the sidewalk. Dad hailed a cab. When it drew up I told him, "Listen, it's okay. You don't need to see me home."

"My meeting can wait, Joey. I'll phone from the call box on the corner when we get—home. I'll tell them I got tied up a little. They'll wait."

"Listen," I said, "I got all the way down here by myself. I don't need you to take me home."

He stood looking down at me, frowning a little.

"I don't need you," I said.

"You're— sure, son?" He sounded like he didn't know *what* to do.

"Sure I'm sure!" I told him.

I opened the door of the taxi and got in.

My dad handed me five dollars. "Give the driver thirty cents tip," he said. "And keep the rest. For a bonus on your allowance this week." He kind of smiled at me. "I'll get the circus tickets," he said. "For Saturday. That's opening night."

"Okay," I said.

"See you Saturday," he said. He slammed the cab door closed. And he stood there waving while we drove away.

I knelt on the back seat so I could see him longer. His figure got littler and littler.

Did you ever feel too sad even to cry?

4

When I rang the bell my mom opened the front door right away. As though she'd been waiting there for the bell to ring. She was looking right above my head. Like she thought it would be Dad at the door.

Then she looked down to me.

"Did he bring you home?"

"Well," I said, "he had this very important meeting. So I told him not to bother."

I walked on into the apartment. And Mom closed the door behind me, very hard.

She looked nice. Usually she changes into slacks or a kind of saggy housecoat when she gets home from work. But now she still had on her dress, and her face looked pretty. She even had makeup stuff on her eyes.

"How *was* your father?" Mom said.

"Fine."

"Where did you go?"

"To Schrafft's."

I hung up my coat on a hanger instead of just slinging it at the coatrack like I usually do. I figured I might as well practice doing everything good. In case Dad decided to take me up on my offer.

My mom lit up a cigarette. I mean, what was she doing *that* for? She stopped smoking long ago on account of all those cancer commercials on the TV.

Then she sat down on the couch. "Well —what did your dad have to say? I mean —what did the two of you talk about?"

"He's going to take me to the circus. Next Saturday. On opening night."

"I see." She blew out the cigarette smoke. Like she was kind of mad. "Your Aunt Gladys already got tickets for you and me and the girls."

"For opening night?"

Mom stubbed out the cigarette in the ashtray. "No. The girls are too little to

go in the night." She stood up. "I'll go make dinner. I don't suppose you're too hungry. What did you have in Schrafft's?"

"Listen," I told her. "I don't care *who* I go to the circus with. I don't even care if I *go* to the circus!"

"That's okay, Joey," my mom said. "You go with your dad. It'll be nice on opening night." She put both arms around me and kind of hugged my head. We stayed like that for a long time. At least it seemed like a long time. It seemed like neither of us wanted to move. It felt good, her hugging my head like that. As though she was telling me a lot of things she couldn't say with words. I mean, I didn't know *what* she was telling me. But I sort of understood anyway, you know?

Then my mom said, "Well, hungry or not—I guess I better get dinner." And she went into the kitchen.

We ate in the kitchen. We usually do when Dad phones that he's working late and he won't be home for dinner. I mean Mom figures why cart all the stuff into the dining room just for her and me. But this time it was different. Usually when we have dinner in the kitchen Mom reads a magazine or something. And I read a comic book, or sometimes even I do some homework. History or something. And Mom leaves the kitchen radio on so there's music and news while we're eating.

But this time she turned the kitchen radio *off*. And she didn't read. It was like she had planned out that she should *talk* to me at dinner. So she was talking. Not about anything too special. Just about school and how was my teacher. And was that bully, Freddy Nelson, still acting up so much. And which boys did I like best in my class. Things like that.

I didn't feel too much like talking, but I answered all her questions the best I could.

Then the telephone rang.

We both stopped talking. We looked at each other.

My mother shoved back the chair and ran to the telephone.

I *knew* it was my dad. His meeting was over and he was phoning to say he'd be home for dinner.

"Oh — Gladys. Hi."

That *stupid* Aunt Gladys!

I could tell by my mom's voice that she'd thought too it might be Dad.

"Look, Gladys," my mom said, "I don't even want to talk about it now. Maybe tomorrow. I'll call you tomorrow at the office. . . . Okay. *Okay*, Gladys!" And she hung up.

"You forgot to tell her about the circus tickets," I said when my mom came back to the kitchen. "To cancel them."

"Oh—yes," my mom said. "Well, I'll tell her tomorrow. What would you like for dessert, Joey? Raspberry Jell-O or ice cream?"

What kind of ice cream?"

"Burnt almond."

I nodded. We usually had burnt almond. That was my dad's favorite kind.

"I'll take the Jell-O," I said.

The phone rang again. This time I said to myself, *It's not Dad.* I said it over and over while Mom was going to answer it. I didn't want myself to be disappointed again. And I was right. It wasn't Dad. It was one of Mom's friends from the department store where she works.

As a matter of fact the phone rang quite a lot that night. It kept ringing while I was doing my homework. And then, afterwards, while I was watching TV. (I found

I was sticking to my list of promises even though Dad had told me it wouldn't make any difference.)

Mom didn't even notice that I wasn't doing my homework with the TV on. I guess she was too busy talking on the phone to notice anything much. I never knew she had so many friends. It seemed like everyone had heard that my dad had walked out on my mom and me and wanted to find out more about it.

At first she started telling each one that she'd call them back the next day. But then — about the fourth one who called — my mom started talking about it. She said, "Wait a minute, Mary." And she closed the door of her bedroom.

I closed the door of my bedroom, too — because I sure didn't want to hear!

That night I was in bed exactly on the minute of my bedtime. Teeth washed, everything. I felt by now like I was in real training — for in case he came home.

Mom was on the phone again. But she came in when she finished. She seemed kind of surprised to find me in bed with the light out and everything.

"Well," I said, "why shouldn't I be in bed? It's my bedtime, isn't it?"

She knelt down beside me in the dark. "You're a good boy, Joey," she said.

I put my both arms around her neck like I was three years old or something.

"What would I do without you, Joey?" she said very softly.

"Don't worry, Mom," I told her. "Everything'll be okay." Suddenly, all of a sudden, instead of feeling like three, I felt older than she was.

"I love you so much, Joey," she said. "Do you know that?"

"Sure, Mom," I said. "I know."

After a while she kissed me and wiped her cheek along my forehead to wipe off her tears. Then the phone started ringing again. She kind of sighed. Then she got up and left.

"Close the door, please," I called out after her.

So she did.

I lay there hearing over and over in my head how she had said, "I love you so much, Joey. Do you know that?"

I mean I really *believed* that she loved me. And that she wouldn't stop loving me. Maybe she'd even love me more if my dad didn't come back home. I mean, who else would she have to love, except me?

And I remembered the way Dad had said how it would be *terrible* if I hadn't been born. He really meant that. He really did love me—now. But what if he didn't come home any more? What if he kept on living apart from us in some downtown hotel or somewhere? How long would he keep *on* loving me?

Like last summer I went to visit my grandpa in Ohio. And when I was living there—well, you could really say I loved my grandpa a lot. But after I *left* the farm —well, I hardly even thought about him any more. Actually, I missed Mangy, his cat, and Dodo, his nineteen-year-old basset hound just as much as I missed Grandpa. More even.

And after a month I hardly even thought about Mangy or Dodo. And I always found something important I had to do when Mom told me I should write to Grandpa, who was lonely on the farm and loved to hear from me.

Probably, if my dad got the divorce, it would happen exactly like that. He'd forget all about me. Except now and then

maybe he'd think: *Well, it's a pain in the neck, but I guess I better write the kid a little letter.*

Suddenly I started hating my dad. I mean, I'd hated him before. Plenty of times. But not like *this*. It was like my whole self had just turned into solid hateness.

It was *his* fault. My mom wanted him back. I knew that. Why else had she gone to the trouble to put on eye makeup and everything when she thought he was bringing me home from his office?

My *mom* hadn't walked out on me. And she never would.

He had!

He didn't even care enough about me to take me home in the taxi.

I remembered the way he had stood, waving a little, while I drove away.

Then it was like I still kept seeing him when he stepped off the curb. And another taxi came along and knocked him down and ran right over him and he was dead.

I saw him lying there in the street run over and all bloody and dead. And I was standing there looking down at him. I

didn't even feel sorry at all. I said to my-self: *It serves you right.* I didn't say it out loud because that might not sound too polite to say about your own father. But I sure said it to myself. Loud. *IT SERVES YOU RIGHT.*

I sat up.

I rubbed my hands hard over my fore-head like I was trying to wipe it all away. Those things I had just thought.

I felt shaking scared.

Maybe he *would* get run over—just like I'd wished.

Maybe he'd be killed. And it would be my fault.

I hardly ever pray. On my knees, I mean. But I got out of bed, and I knelt down and put my hands in front of my face like the top of a roof. And I prayed out loud.

"Please, God, don't pay any attention to what I just thought. I didn't mean it. I love my daddy. No matter *what* happens. Forget what I said, God. Please! Hey, God, can you hear me?"

5

The next Saturday my mom went to work on the late shift. The store stays open till nine every Saturday night, and she had to work from four till nine. It was very convenient, my mom said, because her store isn't too far from the downtown hotel where my dad's staying.

So she dropped me off there before she went on to work.

I think she had it in her mind to bring me right to my dad's hotel room. At least, riding downtown on the bus she seemed kind of nervous. And she looked very nice, like she was expecting to see him.

When we walked into the hotel lobby

she asked at the front desk for Mr. Joseph Grant's room number.

"Four nineteen," the deskman told her.

We started towards the elevator. Then my mom said, "Maybe I'd better — ring up first."

She sounded scared. That's the only word for it. Her voice was all tight. Not like her voice at all.

Well, if you want to know, I felt scared, too. But I don't know why. I mean — your dad's going to take you to the opening night at the circus. That's nothing to be scared of exactly, is it?

There were three telephones by the wall with a sign above them: HOUSE PHONES. We went over there, and my mom lifted the receiver and said, "Four nineteen, please."

Then she said, "Joe?" — like she was a little surprised to hear him answer. I mean, who did she think would be up there? "It's — us," she said. I mean, that sounded kind of stupid, too. I mean, after all, who did she think he'd think it was?

"Shall we — come up?" she said.

I couldn't hear what my dad answered, but she said, "Yes, I have time. I don't have to be at work till four."

Then she didn't say anything. But she nodded a little. "Well—all right," she said. "If you think it's best that way."

She hung up. She just stood there, holding hard onto the receiver.

Finally I said, "So are we going up or what?"

"Well—*you* are," she said. "He thinks it's better that he and I— Well, not today. He's probably right. I'll just put you in the elevator, Joey. Push for the fourth floor. He'll be there to meet you."

"I don't *want* to go without you, Mom," I told her. "I don't want to go to the stupid old circus. I'm too old for the circus anyway!"

"Well, it's too late now, Joey," she said. "I have to go to work. You'll have fun. You'll see. And remember everything so you can tell me all about it. Okay, Joey?"

We were at the elevator. The door opened. People got out. And then my mom sort of gently shoved me in. "You'll have fun, Joey," she said. More people got in. The elevator door slid closed.

I was so scared it was like I was frozen. I forgot all about pushing the thing for number four. We went right up to twelve and started coming down again.

I was still as scared, but at least I managed to push the 4. When the door slid open, there was my dad. So I got out.

"Well, hi, Joey," he said. "What happened? You went right past this floor."

"Yeah," I said. My heart was thumping so hard I could hardly talk. I mean, what was the matter with me? Who ever heard of being so scared of your own dad? Well, I wasn't scared *of* him exactly. I was just scared.

He put one hand on my shoulder, and we walked down the hotel hallway. It was sort of dark, with a lot of doors. We passed one door where some woman was laughing. She sounded drunk or something. Behind another door someone was playing rock music real loud. I mean, at home my dad *never* lets me play rock music loud. He hates it.

A few doors more, and my dad stopped and took out a key. "Well," he said, "home sweet home away from home."

I just stood there. So he gave me kind of a little shove—the same way as my mom had done to get me into the elevator.

"Go on in, son," he said.

So I walked into the hotel room, and my dad closed the door behind us.

I mean, I don't have much experience with hotel rooms or anything. So I didn't really know what to expect. Maybe it was pretty nice as far as hotel rooms go. But I thought it was—crummy!

There was a bed; a narrow bed. And an armchair. And a bureau. And a bed table with a lamp on it. And that's *it!* I mean it didn't look as if anyone lived there at all. At home my dad isn't too neat. He always leaves his trousers hanging over the chair or something like that. In fact, my mom's always after him about why doesn't he pick up his clothes. But *here*—I mean, nothing! Maybe he straightened the room up before I came. Maybe he thought it would look better that way. But I thought it looked *terrible*.

How could he rather live in a place like this than at home in our nice apartment where he's got his own record player and his books and his own chair and footstool and pipe rack and *every*thing!

"You want to wash up or anything, Joey?" my dad said. He opened a door to the bathroom. I didn't go in. But at least I could see some of his stuff on the shelf above the sink. His shaving mug.

His vitamin pills. His bathrobe hanging on a hook.

"I went before I left home, " I said.

Because I couldn't think of anything else to do I walked over to the window. "What kind of a view you got?" I said. I pulled at the venetian blind cord. The blinds clattered up. I looked out at the courtyard and a lot of windows with all their venetian blinds down. I guess none of these hotel people wanted to be looking in at each other's lives.

"Not much of a view," my dad said. "Next time you come I may have a better room. On the top floor. With a view of the Hudson River."

"That'll be nice," I said.

I wasn't so scared now. Instead I felt all kind of confused. And angry. I mean, so what, even if he *did* fight a lot with my mom—wasn't it better than living in this crummy hotel? I mean, it just seemed so—lonely.

Suddenly, like a shot in my head, I remembered something Dad had said that day in Schrafft's. Somehow, I'd never even thought of it until right now. But it seemed to be the only answer as to why my dad had walked out on us to live in this downtown hotel.

"Even if I get married again" — he'd said — *"nothing will ever change how I feel about you, Joey."*

"Well, son," my dad said, "You hungry? Where would you like to eat?"

"I don't know much about restaurants," I told him. "It's up to you."

"Well," my dad said, "there's a nice little French place around the corner. If you like French food. Sauces and things like that."

Sauces didn't sound too hot, so I shook my head.

"Italian?" my dad said. "There's a place called Victorio's. I eat there quite a lot. It's good, if you like Italian food."

I shook my head. We have spaghetti and meatballs at least twice a week in school. That's enough.

"How's about Chinese?" my dad said. "There's a place a couple of blocks away. Ever try eating with chopsticks?"

"You think you'll get married again?" I said. I didn't even mean to say it. The words just came out before I'd even thought them up.

My dad looked at me. Then he said, "What gave you that idea?"

I shrugged one shoulder. "I was just wondering," I said. "Well, actually, what I was wondering—if you did get married again, I mean who would your wife be?"

"Who?"

"I mean who would she be to me? I mean my—mother, or what?"

"Listen." Dad sat down on the edge of the bed, and he sort of pulled me down beside him. "Listen, son, I'm not thinking of getting married right now. It may happen someday, but—"

"So what would I call her?" I said. "Mother?"

"I suppose you could if you wanted," he said. "But probably you'd feel more comfortable calling her—Barbara, or Maggie, or Betty—or whatever her name happened to be."

"Well, I'll tell you," I said. I stood up and looked at him. "You don't need to worry about what I'd call her. Because I wouldn't ever call her anything at all! Because I wouldn't ever say one word to her. EVER!"

My father smiled a little. He stood up.

"Well, Joey, he said, "we may have lots of things to worry about. But that is one problem we don't have to worry about right now. What you're going to call the new wife I don't even have yet!" He mussed his hand through my hair. "As I see it, son, the present problem on the agenda is to decide where we're going to have dinner tonight."

"How's about Howard Johnson's?" I said.

"Howard Johnson's it is," my dad said. "There's a great Howard Johnson's two blocks over on Broadway. I'll get my coat, son, and we'll be off for our night on the town!"

At dinner we didn't talk about anything personal.

It was like we had made an agreement with each other, without saying anything about it at all.

We talked about school and things like that. He didn't mention Mom even once. By the time dessert came I couldn't think of any more things to discuss. I felt afraid for a minute that he wouldn't want to take me out any more because we'd run out of things to talk about. But then Dad opened the newspaper and turned to the movie pages, and he began reading over the things he might take me to see. "I sure wish they'd make a few more movies fit for children," my dad said.

"Well," I said, "I don't mind if they're not so fit. I'd be interested anyway."

I guess I felt a little happy. It was the first time in my life that my dad had ever gone over a list of movies to figure out what him and me could see together.

The circus was good, too.

But sometimes it seemed there was too much going on all at the same time. Like dancing bears in one ring. And a tiger riding on an elephant's back in the center ring. And in the ring closest to us, some white dogs jumping through flaming hoops. I didn't know which to look at, when.

My dad kept saying, "Hey, watch over *there*, Joey! Look at *that!* Hey, isn't this *great*, son?"

And I kept saying, "Yeah! It's *great*, Dad!"

He seemed more excited than me. Maybe he'd never been to the circus before. I thought about asking him that. But I

decided not to. He might think I was insulting him or something. I mean, what kind of a father is it who never even took his son one time to the circus?

My dad kept buying me stuff to eat. It seemed every time one of those men in white coats passed by shouting "Sugar candeee" or "Eyes cream . . . Getchur eyes creeeeeeeeeam!" my dad would hold up his hand in a signal. Then the man would come over. And I'd have something *else* to get down.

I wasn't the least hungry. After all, I'd had a big dinner. But I didn't want my dad to think I wasn't enjoying myself with him. If he thought *that* maybe he wouldn't take me out any more. So I just kept on shouting, "Look, Dad! Over *there!*" And pointing. And kind of jumping around in my seat, like I was all excited.

And I ate all the stuff he bought for me.

We took a taxi home instead of a subway or bus. I didn't say too much. Because I didn't feel too hot. If you want to know, I was just busy hoping I wouldn't upchuck in the taxicab.

Luckily, I managed to wait until Dad got me home. He only brought me to the elevator. Didn't come upstairs. But I didn't care. All I cared about was holding out till *I* got upstairs.

As soon as Mom answered the bell I rushed right past her. Into the bathroom. And locked the door behind me.

Afterwards, I went right to bed. But even though it was very late, Mom read me a chapter of *Tom Sawyer*. It was *her* idea, too. I liked it, lying there watching my mom with the lamplight shining on her hair. I like the special low voice she uses when she reads to me. It makes you feel everything *must* be all right. Even when you know it isn't.

6

Three nights later my dad came and took part of the house away.

Yeah, that's right. Dad and his friend Al Jarry showed up around seven o'clock when Mom and I were eating supper in the kitchen and having Our Time. (We both decided that instead of the two of us just sitting at the table, her with a magazine and me with a comic book, it'd be better to talk to each other about Things. Sometimes these are just regular things, you know—about homework. Or what color to have the bathroom painted because the guy in the apartment above ours let his bathtub overflow and it spoiled all

76

the paint on our bathroom ceiling and walls. And sometimes we talk about — I mean, things that are hard to talk about. Like — you know, divorce and all that stuff.)

Anyway, right in the middle of Our Time the doorbell rings. The first few days Mom and I always used to jump — inside anyway — when the doorbell rang. Or the telephone. Maybe it was Him. But by this time we had stopped expecting it to be Him. And this time it was!

So in he comes with Al Jarry.

I thought to myself, *What — does he need a protector or something?* But it wasn't that. He needed someone to help him carry out his things.

"Hi, June," he says to Mom in the way of a friendly stranger — like she was someone he'd met that morning.

"Hi," Mom said back. And that was practically the only thing she *did* say to him. I could tell she was mad. I mean, it wouldn't have hurt him to call us up and tell us he was coming. (I noticed, even though she was mad, she went into her bedroom and put on makeup and changed her blouse.)

Meanwhile Dad packed up some books.

A whole bunch of them, in cartons he'd brought with him. When he'd finished, each bookshelf looked like a mouth with a lot of teeth missing.

I stood watching him.

Once Dad said, "Want to help put the books in the carton, Joey?"

"No!" I said in quite a loud, fresh voice.

He didn't talk very much to me after that.

Al Jarry didn't either. He seemed kind of embarrassed being there.

Dad said to him, "Will you pack up the records, Al? You can take them all. Joey keeps his in his bedroom. And June never listens."

I mean, that was kind of a nerve of him. Maybe my mom might want to start listening to music, now that she's alone so much and has more time.

When Mom came out of the bedroom with her makeup on, Dad went in there to pack his clothes. Meanwhile Mom started talking to Al Jarry. Making kind of stiff conversation about how was Jean and the kids.

Only once my dad came out to talk to her, and that was to ask where was the big valise we'd bought when we thought we were going to Florida that summer.

Mom gave him the valise, and he went back and finished packing. Then Dad and Al Jarry carried the suitcases and the cartons and the record player out to the elevator. I followed them out there.

"How're you going to get all that stuff into that little lousy hotel room?" I said to my dad.

He looked at me. "Didn't I tell you, Joey? I got the big room I wanted, on the twelfth floor."

"With a view of the Hudson River?"

"Yeah," Al Jarry said. "If you hang out the window and twist your neck around you can see a little sliver of the river — on a clear day."

My dad laughed. But not like he thought the joke was too funny. Then he said, "Keep the elevator here, Al. I'll just go get the TV." And he walked back into the apartment.

I followed him. "HEY!" I said. "You're not taking our TV!"

My dad turned to me with a big smile on his face. "Joey," he said, "I've got a great surprise for you. Tomorrow after-

noon they'll be delivering to this house the one thing you've always wanted."

"What's *that?*" I said.

"A color TV set!" My dad waited, like he was expecting flashing lights to go off. Or maybe I was supposed to jump up and down and throw my arms around him and scream out: *Gee, Dad, the one thing I've always wanted!*

"It'll be *cable* TV too!" my dad said. "So you'll have a lot more channels to look at. And the picture will always be clear as a bell. No more ghosts. No flip-flops. Great!"

I just stared at him. I didn't say anything. I couldn't! I mean here he walks in at seven o'clock in the night and starts taking part of our house away. And what does he offer to make it all up to us? A color TV set with no flip-flops!

Sure, maybe a couple of times I *had* mentioned to him that it might be nice to watch the ball games in color. But if you want to know, my whole idea was that if the games were in color my dad might be more interested in sitting down and watching them with me. Like Andy Phillips' dad does. (They watch and eat popcorn and drink Cokes and cheer and holler at the umpire and everything. Just like they're really at the ball game.)

Anyway, my dad walked out with our TV set in his arms, and all he said was, "So long, son. See you Sunday."

I didn't even answer him. If you want to know, right then I felt I never wanted to see him again.

My mom was standing by the door. All he said to her was, "So long, June. See you."

She didn't answer either. She just kind of nodded. But when he'd gone out into the hall she gave the door a hard slam behind him.

Then my mom and I went back into the kitchen to finish our supper. But even though it was still Our Time, we didn't talk any more. It seemed like there was just too much to say.

The next afternoon two men came puffing into the house carrying the new color TV set. And an hour later another guy came and attached it up for cable.

They put the set in my mom's room. (I'm trying to get in the habit now. Calling it just—Mom's room.) She asked me if I'd mind if we had the new set in there. She doesn't sleep too good, she said, so she likes to lie in bed and watch the movies late at night.

But I'm allowed to sit on her bed whenever I want to watch my programs. It *is* a lot better watching things in color. And that cable hookup *is* great. Just like my dad said. Perfect reception. No more flip-flops.

But if you want to know, somehow I'd rather have that old black and white set back again.

I look at TV a lot more than I used to. Matter of fact, I sometimes keep it on even when I'm not watching it. Especially after six o'clock. That was when my dad came home from the office—unless he had to work late. Which happened pretty often.

Still, the house does seem extra quiet now after six o'clock. That's how come I leave the TV on, talking. And Mom doesn't ever holler at me to turn it off. Actually, she hasn't hollered at me once for the past three weeks. Far as I can remember, she's never been this nice to me in her whole life. She kisses me a lot. And lets me do pretty much what I want.

Sometimes I'd rather she'd holler at me a little. Like she used to.

And my dad — *he* never hollers at me any more either.

Last Sunday he told me how come.

It was when we were looking at the monkeys.

You know something, my dad never took me to the zoo before. Not as long as I can remember, anyway. Mom did. And sometimes I used to feel kind of jealous — seeing the other kids at the zoo with their dads.

But it's different now. Sounds crazy, but it's true. Now that he isn't at home any more, seems like I see more of him!

Anyway, last Sunday he took me to the zoo, and we were watching the monkeys. One was eating two bananas at once. And another was squatting on a trapeze scratching his behind. My dad and I began laughing. I looked up at him. And he looked down at me and kind of mussed my hair.

Then he said, "It's better this way, isn't it, son?"

"What way?" I said.

My dad scowled. But not as though he

was mad at me. Like he was trying to think of how to say what he was trying to say.

Finally he took my hand, and we walked together to the end of the monkey house. There was no one much looking at the big baboon. No wonder. That baboon was just sitting there staring out like a dummy. We stopped in front of the cage, and Dad stared in at the baboon like it was the most fascinating thing he'd ever seen. And then he said, "The thing is, I'm not all tied up in knots inside anymore. What I mean, I can relax with you now. I can—enjoy you."

But he wasn't looking at me when he was saying all this. It was like he was explaining these kind of inside things to the stupid baboon.

Anyway, I heard him.

7

At first I didn't mention anything about it to anyone. I mean, my dad
living downtown in that crummy hotel.
Him walking out on us and all. I felt—
ashamed. Even though the whole thing
wasn't my fault, maybe people would
think it was.

But one afternoon I was sitting on the
bus next to Pepe Gonzales, and suddenly
I said, "You know why I borrowed that
money from you that day?"

Pepe said, "Why?"

So I told him. I didn't mean to tell
him. As matter of fact, I wasn't planning
to tell anyone—*ever*. I had it all figured

out that when someone came to my house on a Saturday or something, I'd just happen to mention that my dad was at the office.

But, for some reason, I found myself spilling the whole works to Pepe. Right there on the public bus.

And you know what he said at the end? "So what?"

Yeah, he didn't bat an eye. "Lots of kids got no dad living in the house," he said. "There's a boy on my block who doesn't even know who his dad *is!*"

I looked at Pepe, kind of surprised.

"That's right," he said. "This little kid used to tell everyone his dad got killed in a car crash. But one day when we was playing dominoes on his front stoop, he tells me, 'You know, man, maybe my dad got kilt and maybe he didn't. I'll never know, 'cause I never even seen him once. I don't even know who he *is!*' And then this little kid laughed and laughed. We both did."

"Yeah," I said. "That *is* kind of funny. Not even knowing who your dad *is!*" I laughed too. A little bit.

I mean, at least I'll always know who my dad *is.*

When it was time for me to get off the bus I said, "Hey, why don't you get off with me? Maybe you could come for supper or something."

I was expecting Pepe to say No. After all, I am two whole classes younger than him. But he said, "Sure, man. Why not?"

I felt proud bringing him home. And my mom seemed glad too. She's heard plenty about Pepe. I mean he *is* one of the best basketball players in our whole school!

Mom said we were having casserole for dinner. Casserole—that's her fancy name for warmed-up leftovers. But when she saw me sort of scowl she said we could order up what we wanted, like in a restaurant—just so long as it was something she happened to have in the house. Like hot dogs and potato chips, she said.

After he phoned his mother, Pepe and I sat at the table, and Mom put on an apron and pretended to be a waitress. And we ordered four hot dogs each, and lettuce and mayonnaise and a bowl of potato chips. And Cokes. And two ice cream cones each for dessert—one vanilla, one strawberry. (I don't go too much for chocolate chip mint any more.)

After dinner Pepe and I lay down on the living room rug and played dominoes.

Maybe the domino playing reminded Pepe of that kid with no father at all. Anyway, he suddenly said, "You know what, man? Last week we got a letter from my papa in Puerto Rico. He says it'll be two years before he can get to the Mainland. That's here, the Mainland."

"Oh," I said. And I fitted my domino onto the tail of another one on the rug.

"Seems to me," said Pepe, "if he *wanted* to come and live with us he could get himself over here a little quicker than that."

"Your turn," I said.

So Pepe selected out his domino and put it in place. "I was feeling kind of low when I got that news," said Pepe. "So you know what I did?"

"What?" I said.

"I counted up all the kids I knew in school and on my block who have no dad living in the house with them."

"How many did you count?" I said.

"Fifty-three."

Fifty-three!

Here I'd been feeling sorry for myself —like I was the only kid in the world whose dad had left home. And Pepe knew fifty-three! Maybe if *I* started asking around, I'd find another fifty-three. Or *more!*

"We should start a club," said Pepe.

"*Yeah!*" I sat straight up. "That's a great idea!" I don't know if Pepe was trying to be funny or not. But *I* was serious. "A *secret* club!" I said. "No one'll know how to get in it. Except the ones we *invite* in?"

Pepe sat up too. "Man," he said, "you know something? It'll be such a great club that everyone'll be breaking his head wondering how to get theirself invited to be a member. But we'll never tell!"

"You can be the president," I said. "Being it was your idea."

"Okay," said Pepe. "And you be the treasurer. You can collect all the dues."

"How much should we charge for dues?" I said.

We forgot all about finishing the domino game. We kept on talking about our club until Mom came in and said that Mrs. Gonzales had telephoned, and she wanted Pepe home right away. Because it was late.

It *was* late too. I'd missed three of my best TV programs. But I didn't care.

I lay awake a long time, thinking about our Secret Club.

It makes me feel good—thinking about it. And it makes me kind of laugh inside myself. I mean naturally if there's a good secret club going, everyone wants to be a member, right? So there'll be all these kids knocking themselves out trying their best to get into our club. But they won't be able. We'll just play it cool. Tell 'em, "Sorry, man, you don't qualify." And they'll probably never figure out why.

Pepe wanted to have our first meeting this Sunday. To decide on a secret password, and a club name, and all that. But I told him I couldn't make it on Sunday. Saturday, okay, I said. But not Sunday. Because on Sunday my dad is taking me to a ball game.

We won't just be watching the game on TV like Andy Phillips and his dad. We'll be right there in the stadium. Having hot dogs and soda and hollering at the umpire. Who knows, maybe Andy Phillips will see *me* on his TV screen. And my dad.

You know what my dad told me?

No more bowling with The Boys on Sunday! Not any more. From now on every single Sunday will be for me.

Me and him together.

92414

DATE DUE

FE 13 '75	JA 19 '77	JUL 30 '8	MY 11 '85
FE 27 '75	FEB -9 '77	FEB 24 '8	OCT 24 '85
MR 13 '75	MAR 2 '77	MAR 10 '8	DEC 17 '8
MR 16 '75	MAR 31 '77	06 '8	
AP 10 '75	MAR 31 '77	MAY 1 '84	
AP 28 '7	FEB 15 '78	MAY	DEC 21 1988
MY 1 '75		MAY 1 '84	DEC 31 1989
MY 9 '75	MAR 6 '78		DEC 21 1989
MY 15 '75	MAR 18 '78	MY 1 '84	DEC 21 1989
JY 24 '75	APR 25 '78		OCT 2 9 1990
SE 30 '75	MAR 13 '79		
OC 23 '75	DEC 20 '7	MAY 1 '84	DEC 1 2 1990
		APR 2 8 1992	